Salamander Rescue

Pamela McDowell
Illustrated by Kasia Charko

ORCA BOOK PUBLISHERS

Text copyright © 2016 Pamela McDowell
Illustrations copyright © 2016 Kasia Charko

All rights reserved. No part of this publication may be reproduced or transmitted in
any form or by any means, electronic or mechanical, including photocopying,
recording or by any information storage and retrieval system now known or
to be invented, without permission in writing from the publisher.

Library and Archives Canada Cataloguing in Publication

McDowell, Pamela, author
Salamander rescue / Pamela McDowell ; illustrated by Kasia Charko.
(Orca echoes)

Issued in print and electronic formats.
ISBN 978-1-4598-1123-2 (paperback).—ISBN 978-1-4598-1124-9 (pdf).—
ISBN 978-1-4598-1125-6 (epub)

1. Salamanders—Juvenile fiction. I. Charko, Kasia, 1949-, illustrator
II. Title. III. Series: Orca echoes
PS8625.D785S25 2016   jc813'.6   C2015-904534-7
C2015-904535-5

First published in the United States, 2016
Library of Congress Control Number: 2015944562

Summary: In this early chapter book set in Waterton Lakes National Park, Cricket and her friends
help a herd of long-toed salamanders safely migrate across the road to Crandell Mountain.

Orca Book Publishers gratefully acknowledges the support for its publishing programs
provided by the following agencies: the Government of Canada through the Canada Book Fund
and the Canada Council for the Arts, and the Province of British Columbia
through the BC Arts Council and the Book Publishing Tax Credit.

Cover artwork and interior illustrations by Kasia Charko
Author photo by Ellen Gasser

ORCA BOOK PUBLISHERS
www.orcabook.com

Printed and bound in Canada.

19 18 17 16 • 4 3 2 1

For Catherine and James—stay wild.

Chapter One

"Warden McKay?" The radio on the truck's dashboard crackled. "There's a bear jam on Crandell Mountain Road. Can you help? Over."

"Ten-four. How far down the road is the bear?"

"It's in the berry patch, two miles from the campground."

"I'll take care of it. Warden McKay out." He turned to his daughter, Cricket, sitting in the passenger seat. "I bet old Samson is posing for the tourists again. Are you ready for a little adventure, Cricket?"

A bear jam could be a big problem. Tourists loved spotting all the wildlife in the national park. Deer and goats wandered through the village every day. Moose crashed through the campground. And a single bear beside the road could stop traffic for miles.

Warden McKay slowed down when they turned onto Crandell Mountain Road. It was a skinny, rough road that twisted and turned through the hills. There were places for drivers to pull over to take pictures of the scenery. But in a bear jam, people parked anywhere—in the ditches, on the grass and even in the middle of the road!

Sure enough, the road ahead was jammed with vehicles. Tourists leaned out of car windows and stood to look through sunroofs. Everyone had a camera in hand. Everyone was looking up the hill.

Warden McKay turned on the truck's big orange strobe lights and pulled far off the road to park. He hopped out before Cricket could undo her seat belt. He shook his head. "Promise me you'll stay in the truck," he said.

"I can help, Dad. C'mon, I'll be in fourth grade in a few weeks."

"Not this time. I can't be worried about you while I try to get these people back into their cars."

Cricket sighed. As she sat in the truck, a little black bear cub tumbled out of the bushes beside the road.

He stood up and looked at the crowd of people.

"Everyone, please get back into your cars," Warden McKay ordered, trying to get the traffic unsnarled. But the tourists kept snapping pictures.

On the other side of the road, Cricket saw a large bush move. A long black nose poked out. Then a furry head with round ears. It was the mother bear!

No one noticed as the large black bear walked across the ditch toward the cars. The bear spotted a boy leaning out of a car window. He had something in his hand and was calling to her. "Hey, bear, want some lunch?"

"Don't feed her!" Cricket yelled out of the truck window. "Roll up your window, quick!"

The boy looked at Cricket in surprise. The bear stood up on her back legs. She sniffed the air and opened her mouth wide.

The boy closed his window just in time. The mother bear leaned on the car with her front paws and peered in at him. She shook her head. Then she dropped back to the ground and walked around the car to her cub. Together they disappeared into the bushes.

Cricket took a deep breath.

"Good job, Cricket," her dad called, giving her a thumbs-up. "Now, everyone get moving. Come on."

Chapter Two

After dinner that night, Cricket told her best friend, Shilo, about the bear jam.

"And he just stuck his hand out the window to feed the bear?" Shilo asked, shaking her head. "That's crazy." She walked along the top of Cricket's backyard fence until she reached the big poplar tree. She grabbed a branch and swung up into the tree.

"I bet I could jump onto Mr. Tanaka's roof from here," Shilo called down.

"You're crazy! That roof is so old, you'd end up in his living room!"

Shilo laughed. The tree shook as she jumped from branch to branch on her way down to the ground.

"Dad says the cat at the stable had her kittens. Do you want to go see?" Cricket asked.

"Sure!"

The girls jumped on their bikes and pedaled up the long hill on the only road out of the village. As they rounded a corner, they both stopped, surprised to see a woman crouching in the middle of the road. She had a bucket beside her. She lifted something from the road and placed it in the bucket.

Shilo frowned at Cricket.

"Not another wacky tourist," Cricket whispered.

"Remember the woman who picked dandelions for her tea?" Shilo asked, giggling.

Cricket tried not to laugh. "Or the man who scooped elk poop and sold it as organic fertilizer?"

The woman looked up and smiled at them. She wore a vest with lots of bulging pockets, and a ruler poked out of one of them.

"Hello, girls," she said. "It's a nice night for a ride."

Cricket nodded, trying to look into the bucket. "What are you doing?"

"I'm researching these little guys," the woman said. Three tiny salamanders scurried at the bottom of the bucket.

They were the size of Cricket's pointer finger.

"Those are long-toed salamanders!" Cricket exclaimed. "We read about them in Science last year." The salamanders were dark green with yellow splotches and stripes on their backs. On each back foot, the fourth toe stuck out, extra long.

"That's right. I'm studying their migration from the lake to Crandell Mountain. My name is Dr. Pantillo, but you can call me Kate."

"Hi, Dr. Kate. I'm Cricket, and this is Shilo."

"Cricket? That's an interesting name."

Shilo laughed. "Her real name is Jenna. Cricket's just a nickname."

"My grandpa called me Cricket a long time ago, when I collected crickets for a cricket zoo."

Dr. Kate smiled.

"Salamanders are cool," Shilo said. She liked slippery things, like toads and snakes.

"Look, there's another one over there," Cricket said, pointing farther down the road.

"Uh-oh, a seagull has spotted him," Shilo said.

"Hey!" Cricket shouted as the seagull hovered over the salamander.

"He's not your dinner!" Shilo yelled, waving her arms until the seagull took off.

Dr. Kate hurried over, picked up the salamander and gently placed it in her bucket. The girls followed her across the road to the long grass at the foot of Crandell Mountain. A car with a canoe strapped on top went whizzing past them.

"This road is really dangerous for an animal that small," Cricket said.

"Yeah, at least people slow down for a deer or a bear," Shilo said. "But they can't see salamanders on the road."

"That's part of the problem for sure," Dr. Kate said, digging a notebook and pen from one of her pockets.

"Problem? What's wrong with the salamanders?" Cricket asked.

"There are only two species of salamander here in Alberta," Dr. Kate said as she wrote something down. "They aren't endangered or threatened, but Waterton's population of long-toed salamanders is getting smaller every year."

"So that's why you're here," Shilo said.

Dr. Kate nodded. "I'm looking for reasons why the salamanders are dying." She tipped the bucket, and the salamanders slid into the grass.

"Can we help you with your research?" Cricket looked at Shilo.

"Maybe tomorrow? We're going to the stable to see the new kittens right now."

"Sure. I'll be here," Dr. Kate said.

"Let's go before it gets dark." Shilo hopped onto her bike. As the girls raced off for the stable, Cricket worried about the salamanders.

"Hey, Peaches, did you go out for a ride today?" Cricket asked, laying her bike on the grass near the corral. A little palomino horse nickered and walked over to have her ears rubbed. Peaches was Cricket's favorite.

Moses, a big gray horse, stretched his head over the fence. He blew hot breath on Shilo's neck and bumped her helmet.

"Careful, silly—you'll get horse drool on me." Shilo plucked a dandelion and offered it to him. He took it carefully between his bristled lips and chewed noisily.

"Cricket, look," Shilo said, pointing across the road. "That must be her."

Cricket turned in time to see a black-and-white cat with a tiny kitten in her mouth disappear through the barn door. "That's one way to get an animal across the road."

"Too bad it won't work for salamanders."

The girls peeked inside the quiet, dark barn. Cricket squeezed through the door. She saw a flash of white near the hay bales.

"Do you see her?" Shilo whispered.

"She's back here. Are you coming?"

"Um, no. I'll just wait here." Shilo stayed at the door. As tough as Shilo was, she didn't like the dark at all.

Cricket found the mother cat with four black-and-white kittens curled up between two hay bales. The mother purred. The kittens mewed and wiggled. Their eyes were still closed.

"They are so little!" Cricket exclaimed when she joined Shilo at the door. "Next time we'll bring a flashlight so you can see them."

The two friends slid the heavy barn door closed and said goodnight to Peaches and Moses. They hopped on their bikes and sped down the hill into the village.

Chapter Three

"I had a dream about salamanders last night," Shilo said. She was hanging upside down from the monkey bars at the playground on the edge of Waterton Lake. "Killer seagulls kept swooping down on them, and all I had was a water gun."

"Sounds more like a nightmare," Cricket said.

"Yeah. Mom says I have crazy dreams because I eat pepperoni before bed."

Cricket watched the crowd across the street. Pat's Garage was on the busiest corner in the village. You could buy or rent just about anything at Pat's Garage. Tourists were already lined up to rent mopeds and four-wheeled pedal bikes. Each bike had a bench seat, a canopy for shade and a steering wheel with a horn. Sometimes Pat let Cricket and Shilo drive them for free if business was slow, but today Waterton was full of tourists.

"Hey, there's Tyler." Cricket's older brother disappeared into the garage. "I bet he's getting ice cream. Come on."

Shilo flipped down from the monkey bars and they crossed the street. Pat sold only four flavors of ice cream, but he always served the biggest scoops.

The girls snuck up behind Tyler. "Can we have some too? Please?"

Tyler groaned. "How did you know I was here?"

"Hey, Cricket! Hey, Shilo!" Tyler's best friend, Will, popped up from behind the ice-cream counter. His dad owned Pat's Garage. "What can I get you?"

"Gee, I don't know," Cricket said, pretending to make a tough decision. She *always* picked chocolate.

Once they had their ice-cream cones, the girls crossed back to the playground and sat on the swings. Tyler and Will walked slowly while they licked their ice cream. They were looking for flat round stones to skip on the lake. Rocks filled their pockets.

"How come we've never seen those salamanders before?" Cricket asked. "Do you think they're more endangered than Dr. Kate knows?"

"Maybe they only come out at dusk," Shilo suggested. "Night's a safer time for them to cross the road, that's for sure."

"I guess, but there are still cars on the road late at night. And owls and cats would spot them easily. It's still a pretty dangerous trip."

"What salamanders?"

"What's dangerous?"

Tyler and Will stopped looking for rocks and climbed onto the teeter-totter beside the girls.

"There's a scientist studying the salamanders on the road between Linnet Lake and Crandell Mountain," Cricket said.

"Really? I've never seen salamanders there. Lots of frogs in the marsh, but no salamanders," Will said. "Why are they on the road?"

Shilo looked at Cricket. She shrugged.

"They must be migrating." Tyler was going up and down on the teeter-totter with his ice-cream cone in one hand and rocks in the other. "Salamanders have to lay their eggs in water. Now they've hatched, and they're going to hibernate on Crandell Mountain."

Will looked doubtful. "Tiny salamanders climb Crandell Mountain? Really, Tyler?"

Tyler laughed. "Not all the way to the top! They just need a drier spot for their burrows."

"Let's go back tonight to help, Cricket." Shilo looked at the boys. "Do you guys want to come too?"

Tyler paused the teeter-totter, leaving Will sitting high above the ground. "Sure, I'll help."

"Um, Tyler? Don't put me down, okay?" Will was looking over at the trees on the edge of the playground. A mother deer stood a few feet away. Two fawns bounced out of the trees, playing.

The kids froze and watched as the fawns passed underneath Will's feet. The mother deer froze too. Her wet, black nose quivered. She stamped a front foot. Would she charge to protect her fawns? Cricket held her breath.

She stamped again, and the fawns bounded away toward the lake. The mother deer flicked her tail and followed them.

"Okay, Tyler, you can put me down now," Will said, keeping his eyes on the deer family.

"That was close, you guys," Cricket said. "I thought you were going to drop your ice-cream cones."

"Not a chance." Tyler opened his fist. "I didn't even drop my skipping stones."

Shilo groaned. "You guys have rocks in your heads."

Chapter Four

"I hoped you would come tonight," Dr. Kate said as Cricket, Tyler and Shilo rode up on their bikes. She was crouching in the middle of the road and held out extra buckets she had brought for them. Cricket introduced Tyler to Dr. Kate, and then they all got to work.

"If you can collect the salamanders, I'll measure and mark them for my research," Dr. Kate said. "We'll let them go in the grass on the other side of the road, like last night."

During the day the road had been busy with lots of tourists and traffic, but by evening things were quiet. Hikers were resting their tired feet. Fishermen were in their cabins, cleaning their catches. Campers were cooking their dinners over fires, and the visitors who had come to Waterton for the day had all left.

"Don't try to grab him by the tail," Dr. Kate warned. "Squeeze him gently between his front and back legs and cup him in your hands. He won't squirm in the dark. Go ahead and give it a try."

"He likes the dark?" Shilo asked in surprise.

Dr. Kate nodded. "He feels safer in the dark, so he's calmer."

"Lucky him."

Cricket crouched down. The salamander at her feet was as long as her pointer finger but thicker. A bright-yellow stripe raced down his back. She took a deep breath and grasped the salamander around his middle. He wasn't slimy, like she'd expected, and he weighed almost nothing. He felt kind of smooshy—like wobbly Jell-O. The salamander's feet felt like tiny twigs scratching the palm of her hand. It tickled.

"Okay, I've got one!" Cricket walked to the side of the road where Dr. Kate had spread out her equipment.

"Great work, Cricket."

While Cricket held the salamander still, Dr. Kate measured him with her ruler. She made notes on her clipboard. Then she prepared a needle.

"What's that? Are you giving him a shot?" Cricket asked.

Tyler came over to watch.

"Kind of," said Dr. Kate. "It's a little dot of blue dye that we put under his skin, where it can't wash off. It helps us count the salamanders."

"Good idea," Tyler said. "That way you'll know if there are fifty salamanders crossing the road or just one little guy going back and forth fifty times."

Dr. Kate laughed. "That's right. The dye won't last forever, but I like it better than some of the other ways of marking salamanders."

"Like what?" Tyler asked. "Couldn't you just take a picture of each one? I bet you could tell them apart by the stripes down their backs. I think they do that with orcas near Vancouver Island."

Dr. Kate nodded. "You're right. Their stripes are unique, just like an orca's fin or a human fingerprint, but I would need a computer program to sort that out. Still, that's better than chopping off one of their toes."

Cricket and Tyler gasped.

"That's so mean!" Shilo said. She had another salamander cupped in her hands.

"Some scientists say it doesn't hurt the salamander, but nature gave them two long toes for a reason. I don't think we should cut them off." Dr. Kate finished marking the salamander in Cricket's hands. "You can put him in the grass now, Cricket."

Tyler tried to help, but holding a salamander in his hands gave him the creeps. He wandered down the road, studying the cement curb the construction crew had built a few months before.

Cricket and Shilo worked steadily, but there seemed to be more salamanders than the night before. Shadows on the road grew longer, and the air cooled.

"It's nearly dark, Cricket. I have to go. Are you coming?" Shilo asked.

Cricket looked at all the salamanders still on the road. "No, I'm going to stay and help."

"Okay, see you tomorrow."

It was completely dark by the time Dr. Kate and Cricket finished. As Dr. Kate packed up her equipment, Cricket looked around for Tyler. He was crouched at the curb, digging into his pockets.

Cricket rolled her eyes. "Don't you have enough rocks, Tyler?"

"Nope." He pointed to a small rock ramp that he had built over the curb. "I call it the Salamander Step." Dr. Kate joined them and watched as a salamander easily climbed the ramp instead of trying to pull itself over the steep curb.

"That's brilliant, Tyler!" Dr. Kate said.

Cricket couldn't believe it. Tyler had finally found a purpose for all those rocks he carried around.

Chapter Five

The next night, all of the stones from the Salamander Step were gone.

"What happened?" Cricket asked, walking up and down the curb, looking for the ramp Tyler had built the night before.

"The rain this morning must have washed the rocks away," Tyler said.

"Or cars could have scattered them," Shilo suggested.

"Well," Tyler said, shrugging his shoulders, "I guess it wasn't such a great idea after all."

"No, it was a wonderful idea," said Dr. Kate. "A permanent Salamander Step would be a great solution, but I'm not sure how we could do that." She handed each of them a recycled bucket from the Pizza Palace.

"I wish there was something more we could do to help," Cricket said.

"We are," Shilo said, picking up three salamanders at the bottom of the steep, smooth curb. They were too tired to try climbing it anymore.

"Let's get these little guys measured and marked as quickly as possible," Dr. Kate said. "They need to get into the cool grass."

It was easy to pick up the tired salamanders because they hardly squirmed at all. But Cricket worried that maybe some of them wouldn't survive.

"Long-toed salamanders are pretty sensitive," said Dr. Kate. "There are all kinds of things that can harm them, not just birds or cars or this new curb."

"Like what?" Shilo asked.

"I bet the salt is bad for them," Tyler said.

Dr. Kate nodded. "Only a little salt stays on the road until summer, but it's enough to irritate a salamander's moist skin. And there are other chemicals on the road and in the water that are bad too," she said.

"I wouldn't want to swim in a lake full of chemicals!" Shilo said.

"Neither do you, right, big guy?" Cricket said, holding a tiny salamander up close to her face.

Everyone laughed. They continued working until it was almost dark and Shilo had to leave.

"Is your friend not allowed out after dark?" Dr. Kate asked as she watched Shilo pedal away on her bike.

"She just doesn't like the dark," Cricket answered. "Oh, Dr. Kate, look!" Dozens of salamanders were creeping out of the grass.

"This is exciting. I think we're getting pretty close to the peak of the migration," Dr. Kate said.

Chapter Six

All night long Cricket tossed and turned. Her dreams were filled with salamanders. They piled up at the curb while she and Shilo scooped them up with their bare hands.

In the morning Cricket was almost too tired to eat breakfast.

"How's the salamander project going?" her mom asked as she buttered a stack of toast.

"Great, except for that new curb."

Warden McKay frowned. "Is there something wrong with it?"

"It's a good curb for the road and the cars, but not for salamanders. It's too steep for them to climb," Cricket explained. "Tyler used rocks to build a ramp that worked for one night, but we need something more permanent. If we had enough money to buy some cement, maybe we could build a proper ramp before the big migration."

Cricket held her breath. She knew that in Waterton, the park wardens made a lot of important decisions. If her dad said no, they would have to think of another idea.

"We know where they like to cross the road," she said. "So we could build the Salamander Step in that exact spot."

"Well, it sounds like a good project, if it doesn't cause problems for cars. But how will you raise enough money?"

"You could sell lemonade," her mom suggested. "Remember last summer when you and Shilo had a lemonade stand? You made a lot of money—almost twenty dollars."

Cricket nodded slowly. It had taken them the whole summer to make that much money. Could they do it in just one day?

An hour later the girls had a plan. Cricket would set up a small table and chairs at the park across from Pat's Garage. Shilo would bring the lemonade and cups and a couple of sandwiches for their lunch.

"How much should we charge for a cup of lemonade?" Shilo asked. "We need to make a bunch of money."

"But if we charge too much, we won't sell any," Cricket said.

"How about twenty-five cents a cup? We'll need to sell a hundred cups to make twenty-five dollars. Do you think we can sell that much in a day?"

"I sure hope so. The salamanders need that ramp right away."

Chapter Seven

The girls set up the lemonade stand in a cool spot in the shade of a big tree. They sold six cups of lemonade right away. But after that, nothing.

"How's business?" Tyler asked, crossing the street from Pat's Garage. The parking lot bustled with tourists waiting to rent mopeds and bikes.

"Terrible," Cricket moaned. "Nobody even sees us over here. There's no way we'll make enough money to buy the cement today."

"Hmm. I'll be right back," Tyler said, turning around and going back across the street. "Just don't go anywhere. The stand is perfect right where it is."

Shilo looked at Cricket and shrugged.

"Come back with some money for lemonade!" Cricket yelled.

"I'll come back with something even better!" Tyler said as he disappeared into Pat's Garage.

A half hour passed, and the girls still hadn't sold any more lemonade. Then Tyler and Will came out of Pat's. They were grinning and carrying big posters.

"This should help you make some money," said Tyler, turning his poster so the girls could see it.

SAVE OUR SALAMANDERS was painted in big green letters. Underneath that was a goofy-looking salamander with a yellow stripe down his back. He was drinking a cup of lemonade.

"Look at mine," Will said. His poster was decorated with two long-toed salamanders juggling bright-yellow lemons. Underneath them it said LEMONADE 25¢ A GLASS.

"That's great, you guys," Shilo said.

"And my dad said you could borrow this." Will handed Cricket a giant bear-bell.

She shook it, and it made a loud, musical sound. A few of the tourists across the street turned and looked at the kids.

"It works!" Cricket said, ringing the bell loudly while the boys put up their signs.

Immediately a group of tourists walked across the street to see what was going on. Soon the table was surrounded by hot and thirsty customers who were all curious about the salamanders.

"I didn't know Waterton had salamanders. What kind of salamanders are they?"

"What are you going to use the money for?"

"Why do the salamanders need saving?"

"Do the salamanders really have long toes?"

Cricket and Shilo tried to remember everything they had learned from Dr. Kate as they answered questions and served lemonade. Tyler looked after the money. Will refilled the jugs and got more cups.

Even local people stopped to see what the fuss was all about. Everyone was interested, and everyone wanted to help.

Chapter Eight

By late afternoon all the lemonade was gone.

"I think we sold a cup of lemonade to every person in the village," Tyler said.

"Uh-uh," Shilo said, shaking her head. "More! I sold three cups to Mr. Tanaka."

"So did I!" Will said. "He must really like our lemonade."

Cricket opened up the money box and organized the coins into stacks, filling the whole table.

"Sixteen," Cricket said, counting carefully. "Is that right?"

Shilo recounted the stacks of coins. "Yup. Sixteen dollars. That's almost as much as we made all last summer," she said in amazement.

Tyler and Will high-fived.

"Let's see how much cement we can buy," Cricket said.

They piled everything in Shilo's wagon and crossed the street to Pat's Garage.

"Well, how was business today, kids?" Pat Watson's voice boomed from the back of the store. "Did you make enough money to rescue our salamanders?"

"We sure hope so, Mr. Watson," Cricket said. "It depends on how much cement costs."

Four bags of cement lay on the floor in the back corner of the store, between jugs of motor oil and a dusty old boat anchor.

"Ten dollars a bag," Mr. Watson said.

"Oh." Cricket's smile faded. "I guess we can only afford one bag."

"Well, how much money did you make?"

"Sixteen dollars," Shilo said.

"Well, you're in luck, because there's a discount for the Salamander Rescue Society. Two bags for sixteen dollars," Mr. Watson said.

"There's only one problem, Dad," Will said. "We have to pay you with sixty-four quarters."

Pat laughed and packed the cement into the wagon, along with a few buckets and a shovel. He handed Cricket a pair of thick rubber gloves, a mask and safety goggles. "Be sure to read the instructions carefully," he said. "And good luck!"

The kids took turns pulling Shilo's wagon with the cement and supplies all the way to Salamander Hill. But Dr. Kate wasn't there.

"Hey, we beat her here," Tyler said.

"Well, we're pretty early," Cricket said. "The salamanders don't start to cross the road until it's nearly dark."

Tyler and Will unloaded the cement.

"If we build the ramp now," Cricket said, "do you think it will be ready for the salamanders to use tonight?"

"I hope so." Tyler picked up two of the smaller buckets. "We'll go get some water from the lake while you open the bags."

Warden McKay stopped by as Cricket and Shilo were studying the instructions on the bags. He placed bright-orange pylons on the road to alert drivers of the construction project.

Shilo giggled as Cricket pulled the safety goggles down over her eyes. "You look like a mad scientist," she said. "Do you really need to wear all that stuff?"

"Absolutely," Warden McKay said. "Cement is corrosive, which means it could irritate or burn your skin and eyes.

And you really don't want to breathe it in either." He put on gloves and a mask and helped Cricket dump the bags into the buckets. Then his radio crackled with news about a porcupine at the post office, and he headed back to his truck.

"Thanks, Dad," Cricket said. She stirred the heavy, gritty mixture while Tyler added water.

"How do we know when it's ready?" Shilo asked.

Tyler looked at the instructions on the bag. "It's supposed to look like thick oatmeal."

"Great. I haven't had oatmeal in a long time." Shilo stepped back. "Does that look about right?"

"It looks good to me," Tyler said.

"Me too." Cricket dug into the cement with a small shovel. "Let's start building."

Traffic drove slowly past the kids as they worked. Curious tourists watched them through their car windows. Many people smiled and waved. Warden McKay checked on their progress again as he drove back into the village.

In an hour the ramp was finished, and the kids went home for dinner. Cricket could hardly eat. What if the cement didn't harden in time? What if Dr. Kate was wrong, and they had missed the big migration?

Chapter Nine

A cool, misty rain was falling as Cricket and Tyler pedaled back up the road. They had finished dinner quickly, and Cricket had thrown a few special supplies into her backpack before they raced out the door.

Dr. Kate wasn't there yet, and neither were Shilo and Will. But the salamanders sure were.

"Wow, Cricket," Tyler said, jamming on his brakes and skidding to a stop. "Look at all of them!"

Salamanders scurried across the wet road. Salamanders crawled from the grass by the lake. Salamanders scrambled up the new ramp.

"It works, Tyler! Your Salamander Step works!"

Cricket and Tyler parked their bikes under a tree to keep dry. Dusk was falling quickly. More and more salamanders darted across the road and used the ramp to get over the curb.

"Wow!" Dr. Kate said when she hiked up the hill and saw the ramp. "Did you kids do this?"

"We sure did," Shilo said, riding up with Will.

"Well, it's fantastic!"

Cricket opened her backpack and gave everyone a flashlight. "And this is for you," she said, handing Shilo a light with a strap to fit over her hat. "You turn it on here," she said, clicking a switch.

Shilo's headlamp lit up the wet road. "Look!" she said.

The road was alive! It quivered and wiggled as hundreds of salamanders scurried toward the mountain.

"The rain must have triggered the migration," Dr. Kate said. "Good thing I brought extra buckets. Look at all the babies!"

All different sizes of salamanders scurried at their feet. There were big ones as thick as Cricket's thumb and skinny ones smaller than her baby finger.

The kids stood beside Dr. Kate and watched the migration. There was no

way they could trap, measure and mark every salamander—there were just too many! Some salamanders had missed the ramp and were stuck, piling up on each other as they tried to scramble over the curb.

"Come on, everyone. Let's give them a lift," Dr. Kate said as she gently scooped some salamanders up and over the curb with her hands.

Suddenly the rumble of a truck engine shook the air. It was a deep rumble that Cricket could feel vibrating in her chest. It must be a big truck! Salamanders covered the road. There was no room for a big truck to drive around them. They had to do something quickly before the truck killed hundreds of salamanders.

Chapter Ten

"Shilo, can you get those pylons back onto the road?" Cricket grabbed her flashlight. "We have to stop that truck." She ran up the side of the road and waved her flashlight back and forth to get the driver's attention as he came around the corner. Shilo and Will carried Warden McKay's bright-orange pylons out to block the road.

The truck slowed down quickly. It stopped four houses away and rumbled like a bear. Its headlights shone on Cricket like a giant spotlight. It was the big rig that delivered ice cream and milk to the businesses in the village.

"Hey!" The driver stuck his head out of the truck's window. "What's going on here? What's that all over the road?"

"Hi, Mr. Dharwa," Will called. "It's the salamander migration. We could use your help." Will offered Mr. Dharwa a bucket as he climbed out of his truck. The big rig blocked the road, and soon a line of cars was parked behind it. People got out of their cars to help.

Cricket wasn't surprised to see the flashing orange lights of her dad's Park Warden truck.

"This is quite a big job, Cricket," her dad said.

"It is," Cricket said. "Dad, I want you to meet Dr. Kate."

"These kids have been a great help," Dr. Kate said, shaking hands with Cricket's dad. "They built the Salamander Step just in time too."

The ramp was covered with salamanders. Nearby, a bucket brigade of people helped lift more salamanders over the curb and take them to the grass.

"The Salamander Step works, but it's not wide enough," Cricket said. "You know what we really need, Dad?"

Warden McKay shook his head.

"A tunnel. If the salamanders could go under the road, they would be protected from cars *and* birds *and* salt."

"A tunnel would solve all the problems," Shilo nodded.

Warden McKay looked from the mountain to the lake. "That's a really big project," he said.

"But a great idea," Dr. Kate added.

"I guess we would need to raise lots more money," Shilo said.

"We'd probably need a whole construction crew," Tyler said.

"We could write a letter to the government," Cricket suggested.

"I could write one too," said Dr. Kate.

"And we could start a petition," Cricket said. "I bet all these people here would sign it. Who wouldn't want to save the salamanders?"

"I would sign that petition, Cricket," Mr. Dharwa said, holding a bucket of salamanders.

"If there's a way to save these salamanders, Cricket, I know you kids can do it," Warden McKay said.

Yes, they could. And they had a whole year before the next migration to make it happen.

Epilogue

In spring 2008, the Alberta government installed tunnels under the road into Waterton. Fences were built to direct the salamanders into the tunnels. Holes in the top allow air, moisture and light inside. These "amphibian underpasses" are not only used by long-toed salamanders. Motion-activated cameras have photographed many animals in the tunnels, including western toads, red-sided garter snakes, tiger salamanders—and even rabbits!

Researchers continue to study this threatened population of salamanders within Waterton Lakes National Park. The salamanders are measured and marked. This information will help researchers estimate their population and track their movements so the salamander habitat can be properly protected.

Why all this fuss over such a tiny creature? Salamanders and other amphibians are highly sensitive to environmental changes. They absorb water and air through their skin, which means other chemicals, like chlorine and salt, can be absorbed as well. If scientists discover something wrong with a population of amphibians, there is probably something wrong with the environment. Finding these problems early can help scientists protect the environment as well as the animals and humans in it.

Pamela McDowell's first career was in education, teaching junior high and high school. She has written more than forty nonfiction books for children. Pamela grew up in Alberta and enjoys writing about the diverse animals and habitats of her home province. *Salamander Rescue* is her second book in the Orca Echoes series. Pamela lives in Calgary, Alberta, with her husband, two kids and an Australian shepherd. For more information, visit www.pamelamcdowell.ca.

Also by
Pamela McDowell

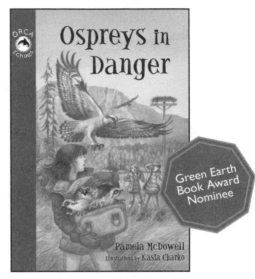

Green Earth Book Award Nominee

9781459802834 • $6.95 PB • Ages 7–9
9781459802841 (pdf) • 9781459802858 (epub)

Can Cricket reunite three baby ospreys
with their parents without a place
for them to build a nest?

"An exciting tale for young animal lovers."
—*School Librarian's Workshop*

ORCA BOOK PUBLISHERS
www.orcabook.com • 1-800-210-5277